Go Away Worries!

Put Them in

The Worry Jar

Michelle White, PhD
Illustrated by Megan D. Wellman

FERNE PRESS

Go Away Worries! Put Them in The Worry Jar
Copyright © 2014 by Michelle White
Layout and cover design by Jacqueline L. Challiss Hill
Cover photo by Eric Yankee
Illustrations by Megan D. Wellman
Illustrations created with pen and ink
Printed in the United States of America

Summary: Caleb's teacher helps him discover a way to deal with his everyday worries.

Library of Congress Cataloging-in-Publication Data
White, Michelle
Go Away Worries! Put Them in The Worry Jar
Michelle White–First Edition
ISBN-13: 978-1-938326-17-2
1. Juvenile fiction. 2. Elementary school. 3. Preoccupation.
4. Feelings and emotions.
I. White, Michelle II. Title
Library of Congress Control Number: 2013947960

FERNE PRESS

Ferne Press is an imprint of Nelson Publishing & Marketing
366 Welch Road, Northville, MI 48167
www.nelsonpublishingandmarketing.com
(248) 735-0418

Dedication

To everyone who needs to find a place for their worries.
Especially to Aaron for being the first one to believe.

I'd like to thank my family and friends for their support
and belief in *Go Away Worries!*

Thanks to Kris Yankee and Marian Nelson from Nelson
Publishing & Marketing for making *Go Away Worries!* a
dream come true.

Thanks to Megan D. Wellman for bringing *Go Away Worries!* to life.

Chapter 1

"Time for the math test!" the teacher said.

Caleb looked around the classroom and watched the other kids get ready. Matt, Caleb's best friend, sharpened his pencil in the front of the room. Jen read a book at her desk; she always read whenever they had a break. Taylor went desk to desk and passed out the multiplication test. Caleb wrote his name at the top as soon as he had his. When he looked up, he freaked out when he saw everyone looking right at him! The kids whispered to each other. Some of them laughed. Some of them pointed.

"Please stop," he whispered.

The teacher stood at the front of the room with the stopwatch, looking at him too. She didn't tell the class to stop laughing because she was also laughing. He dropped his pencil on the floor so he could go under his desk to hide his tears. Before he had a chance to get back up, she started the test.

"Go!" the teacher yelled.

Wait! Wait for me! Caleb thought to himself.

Caleb slowly answered the first few problems and looked around. Everyone was working. He got to the end of the row and sat frozen. He couldn't concentrate. Caleb was afraid to look up. One by one as the other kids finished, they stared at him. Again, they started to whisper to each other.

"He's still working."

"What's the matter, Caleb? Don't you know the answers?"

Leave me alone! His heart raced, and he started to panic. *Don't cry...don't cry!*

When he looked down at his paper, his answers had disappeared.

What? Where did they go?

It kept getting worse. This time when he looked up, everyone stood around his desk.

"What's taking you so long?"

"Come on, Caleb, we're waiting for you!"

"Didn't you study?"

"You'll never be as fast as us!"

Caleb's eyes filled up with tears. "Stop! Please stop."

"You're the last one AGAIN!"

"Just give up, you can't do it."

Stop! Leave me alone!

He covered his ears so he didn't hear them. They teased and made fun of him until Caleb ran out of the classroom.

He heard footsteps coming down the hallway, so he quickly turned and ran the other way—toward the cafeteria. When he opened the doors, he searched for a place to sit and calm down. He pulled out a chair.

"You can't sit here," said a girl. She grabbed the chair from him. He ran to the next table.

"This seat is saved," said a boy.

Caleb couldn't catch his breath because he was filled with so much panic.

Table after table, he was told to go away. He ran out of the cafeteria. With a loud bang, the doors slammed behind him.

Startled, Caleb sat up in bed and rubbed his eyes. His hair was soaked with sweat and his heart beat really fast.

It's just a dream. A bad dream.

He looked at the clock on the table next to his bed. It read two o'clock in the morning. It was quiet in his room except for the soft gurgling coming from the fish tank. He concentrated on the sound and tried to relax.

He fell asleep and the dream began again.

It was the end of the day and Caleb sat at his desk, ready to go home. He waited and waited, but didn't hear his bus number called.

Did I miss it?

All of the other kids were gone. His teacher had her bag over her arm. She turned off the lights and left the room as if he wasn't there. Caleb panicked.

"Wait for me! I'm still here!" he yelled.

She kept walking as if she didn't hear him. He ran after her, but she was gone. Then he ran downstairs and when he looked out the front doors, he saw his bus leaving without him.

"Wait...wait...!" he yelled. "Please, come back! Come back!"

Caleb sat in the middle of the sidewalk, hung his head, and cried.

A familiar voice called his name.

"Caleb. Caleb, wake up," the voice said.

Startled, Caleb sat up in bed. "Huh?" he answered and his eyes focused on his mom.

"You were talking in your sleep," explained Caleb's

mom. "I called your name several times. It's time to get up." She sat on the edge of his bed. "What were you dreaming about?"

"School again," said Caleb. He rubbed his eyes and yawned. "First it was everyone teasing me and then the bus left without me."

"You were dreaming, honey," she said, as she patted his back.

However, Caleb knew she was concerned about him because he'd overheard his mom talking to his teacher last summer. He hid behind the wall and listened to what they were saying. He managed to hear his teacher, Miss White, say, "I might have an idea" before his mom looked at him as he peeked around the corner. They never finished talking because his mom called him over and asked if he was ready to go. Caleb decided he wouldn't make a very good detective.

"Get dressed and come down for breakfast. I made your favorite pancakes," his mom said.

Caleb sniffed the air and tried to forget about the bad dreams. Mom's pancakes were yummy. He smiled and wished they would magically take away his worries.

Chapter 2

Later that day after lunch, Caleb got ready for math. They were having another timed test. He wrote his name at the top of his paper and wiped his sweaty hands on his jeans. For the past twelve Fridays, students in Miss White's fourth-grade math group raced against the timer to show how quickly they could multiply. Caleb wiped his hands again and looked around the classroom.

Miss White stood in front of the room holding the stopwatch that caused Caleb so much worry. To the left, Jen and Taylor were talking quietly at their desks. Matt was making his way from the pencil sharpener to the empty seat next to Caleb. The sun shone through the big windows, warming the classroom, which caused Caleb to sweat even more.

He pushed his sleeves up and waited. Most of his classmates already had their papers upside down, ready to start. It didn't look like anyone else was nervous because they were all talking quietly and laughing.

Looking down at his paper, Caleb replayed the Friday testing in his mind. The farthest he'd made it so far this year was halfway down the paper. Caleb jumped when Matt gave him an elbow to the arm.

"What are you thinking about?" Matt asked.

"Passing this test," admitted Caleb. "I'll never be as fast as you."

Matt laughed. "That's because I'm better than you!" Another elbow made its way to Caleb's arm.

The boys had been friends since second grade when Matt moved to Falcon Elementary School. Matt's dad had a job, opening new restaurants, which caused their family to move around. Before Matt moved here, Caleb never really had a good friend like him. They were best pals, sitting together, playing together, and they were even in karate together. However, this was the first time they were in the same classroom. And not just any room: Miss White's room.

For the past two summers, Caleb went to the science

camp that she taught. The first summer, they learned about space and astronauts. Last summer, she taught them all about chemistry. They made volcanoes, crystals, and even glow-in-the-dark slime. She knew so much and made it so much fun that Caleb knew this was going to be his favorite year yet.

"How did you get so fast?" wondered Caleb.

"I'm just good at it. I don't even have to study," Matt teased.

Caleb wished he could be as fast as his friend.

"All right, everyone ready?" asked Miss White.

Would he answer all of the questions before the timer went off?

"Set?" she continued.

Caleb looked over at Matt. He had his hand lifting up the corner of his paper ready to turn it over and start.

"Go!" called Miss White and she started the timer.

The room was quiet other than the sound of papers flipping over and pencils writing answers. At the end of the first row, Caleb glanced over at Matt. *What?* He was already on the fifth row. *This isn't fair.* As Caleb made it to the second row, some of the other kids started flipping over their papers and putting their pencils down as they were done.

"Yes!" Caleb heard Matt whisper. He was done, too.

Caleb's grip on his pencil tightened as he started on row three. Buzz!

"Pencils down, everyone!" announced Miss White.

Caleb put his pencil down and quickly turned his paper over so no one could see it. He put his head on the desk, closed his eyes, and remembered last night. His mom timed him, and he had nearly finished the entire practice test.

"You can do this, Caleb," she said putting her hand on his shoulder. "Picture yourself on the bottom row, answering your last problem just as the timer goes off."

"Okay, ready," Caleb said hesitantly.

He worked through row after row of math problems and was halfway through the second-to-last row when the timer went off. Caleb smiled when he looked down at his paper. He had almost finished!

"I wish I could do this at school," said Caleb.

"You *can* do this at school," she replied. "Just take a deep breath and imagine it's just you and me sitting in the kitchen."

She was so proud of me last night. Now look how I did!

Caleb knew the answers, but when he got to school, they seemed to be frozen inside his head. As the other kids completed the test, Caleb's mind panicked and stopped working.

What's wrong with me?

Miss White put her hand on Caleb's shoulder and asked, "Are you okay?"

"Yeah, just thinking," Caleb answered.

"Boys and girls, please hand in your tests and take out your reading books," Miss White said, as she continued on her way over to Taylor, who had her hand up.

"How'd you do?" Matt asked Caleb.

Caleb slid down in his chair and slowly turned his paper over. "I'll never finish this test!" he growled. He pushed both of his hands into the pockets of the new sweatshirt that his grandma bought him last weekend.

"That's how I feel about the test for my orange belt in karate," Matt said. "I've taken that test two times already and I keep messing up. I watched you and you make it look so easy. It stresses me out."

"That's because I'm better than you!" teased Caleb, feeling good because it was his turn to beat his friend at something. Caleb got his orange belt two weeks ago. Karate was much easier than math, and Caleb looked forward to going there later that night.

Both boys laughed.

The next morning, Caleb was talking with Zack on his way to the classroom. Zack was also in karate and the fourth grade, but he had Mrs. Daub as his teacher.

"I was so nervous last night, but I finally got it," said Zack. He opened his book bag and pulled out his orange belt. "I brought it to school to show Mrs. Daub."

"Cool," said Caleb.

He felt confident because he was already working on his purple belt. The routines were easy to remember, and Caleb didn't have to think about it much, unlike a lot of the other things that he worried about. If only math facts, and other things, were as easy as karate.

They talked in the hallway outside Miss White's room. "I feel bad for Matt. He tried so hard," said Caleb.

"Yeah, me too," agreed Zack. "Maybe we can help him at recess."

"Good idea," answered Caleb. "We'd better get going. See you later!"

"'Bye, Caleb," said Zack.

As Caleb walked into the classroom, he quickly looked around for Matt. His chair was still on top of his desk. He wasn't at the coat racks or anywhere in the classroom. Worries started to fill Caleb's head.

I wonder where he is. He didn't say anything last night

about not being here.

His classmates were busy either making their lunch choices on the chart at the front of the room or getting their desks ready for the day. Miss White was at her desk doing her teacher stuff, like taking attendance and collecting science homework. Caleb took his chair off his desk and got his science book and notebook out of his book bag. Then he took his homework up to Miss White's desk.

"Good morning, Caleb," said Miss White.

"Good morning. Is Matt here?"

"I haven't seen him yet," she replied.

Caleb began to worry about who he would sit with at lunch. He always sat with Matt. The fourth and fifth graders were allowed to sit anywhere they wanted at the round lunch tables. By the time Caleb's class got down to the cafeteria, the tables were mostly filled, which meant possibly having to sit with kids he didn't know well. He had friends and usually found someone to talk with, but he usually worried until he felt comfortable.

One time last year, when Matt was absent, Caleb sat down next to Kevin.

"Why do you have to sit here?" asked Kevin. "Go away."

Caleb remembered how his stomach felt sick and he didn't know how to answer. So he ended up not saying anything and moved to another table by himself. He kept his head down so nobody could see the tears in his eyes. He didn't eat much of his lunch that day. Kevin made him feel really bad.

"Caleb, are you okay?" Miss White asked. "Caleb?"

"Yeah," said Caleb.

"You look like you were daydreaming about something," she said.

"Oh, I was just wondering where Matt was."

"Maybe he had an appointment, or he doesn't feel well," said Miss White. "Don't worry. I'm sure he's okay."

On his way back to his seat, Caleb saw that Jen's chair was on top of her desk, too.

After the announcements, Miss White explained the science experiment they would do with their partners.

Oh no, I don't have a partner. Caleb felt himself start to panic.

"Taylor and Caleb, would you please work together since both of your partners are absent?" asked Miss White.

That solved one problem.

Throughout the morning, Caleb was so busy that he

almost forgot Matt wasn't in school. That was until he heard Miss White say, "Boys and girls, it's time for lunch."

Suddenly, Caleb didn't feel like eating anymore. His stomach pained, but not from being hungry.

While standing in the lunch line, Caleb could not relax. He didn't know who he would sit with to eat. The cafeteria was filled with loud talking and the lunch lady's voice dismissing classes for recess. The smell of freshly baked pizza hit Caleb's nose and made his stomach rumble. This was his favorite lunch and even though he was hungry, he didn't feel like eating. Once he was through the long line, he saw two tables with empty seats and walked as fast as he could to sit down.

"Caleb, can we sit with you?" asked Taylor and Susie.

"Okay…," muttered Caleb.

Taylor and Susie were nice and Caleb was glad to have someone to sit with, but he didn't feel like talking.

Susie pulled her food and her spelling list out of her pink lunch bag. She began to look over the words as she ate her sandwich. It looked like peanut butter and jelly.

She sighed. "Ugh! These words are hard."

"I know! I didn't do well on the last two tests," admitted Taylor. "I'm worried about my grade. My parents expect As and I only have a B."

Hmmm…I guess I'm not the only one who worries about tests, he thought.

Caleb was glad he didn't have to worry about spelling. He aced the last five tests. Last year he'd won his classroom spelling bee. Caleb smiled as he remembered that day in his head. The winning word was "believed" and he spelled it with ease. As a matter of fact, the certificate he won still hung on his refrigerator at home. His parents were so proud of him.

Caleb left the table to throw his trash away and when he returned, the girls were talking about nail polish. It was a good thing he was able to go outside for recess so he didn't have to hear about all of those girly things. But with Matt gone, he still didn't have anyone to play with, so Caleb walked around by himself until it was time to line up.

Caleb began to worry about finding a seat again, but this time it was on the bus.

I wonder where Kim will be sitting. Will there be an empty seat in the front?

As he stood in line to get on the bus, Caleb could not relax. He watched the back of Kim's head. She was four kids in front of him. She stood a couple inches taller than everyone else. Caleb saw her touch the back of the boy's head standing in front of her. His name was Lucas and he was only in second grade. Lucas rubbed his head. Kim kept doing it again and again, picking and picking on him. Caleb tried to stay as far away from her as he could so she wouldn't pick on him. Once she was on the bus, Kim went directly to the backseat. Caleb sat right behind the bus driver.

"Hi, Caleb. How was your day?" Frank, the bus driver, asked.

"Okay," answered Caleb, not wanting to let him know how it really went.

All of a sudden, Kim's voice boomed throughout the bus, "You have cooties!" She was at it again.

I wonder who the victim is today.

Caleb sank down in his seat and glanced across the aisle.

"She's mean," sighed Lucas, sinking down in his seat too.

"Tell me about it," Caleb agreed, shaking his head.

"Enough, Kim," yelled Frank. "If I have to talk to you again, you'll move to a seat up front."

Lucas and Caleb looked at each other in terror.

It was a relief to know that someone else was also worried about Kim.

When the bus got to Caleb's stop, he was so glad to get off before Kim ended up sitting next to him.

"Good luck," Caleb told Lucas.

The bus pulled away and Caleb felt bad for little

Lucas. Kim was in fifth grade. She should pick on some-body her own size. He rushed to the house to call Matt to see why he wasn't at school.

"Hello," answered Matt's mom.

"Can I talk to Matt?" asked Caleb.

"Hold on," she replied and yelled for him.

"Hello," said Matt.

"Where were you today?" Caleb asked.

"Hi, Caleb. I was at the dentist and, trust me, I would've rather been at school. I had two cavities filled. After that I didn't feel too good to go to class," he explained.

By the time Caleb hung up the phone, he felt a little relieved from his stressful day knowing where Matt had been.

That night Caleb fell asleep before nine o'clock. He was exhausted.

Chapter 3

In the morning, Caleb walked into the classroom and saw his best friend sitting at his desk.

This day was turning out pretty well considering Kim wasn't on the bus and Matt was back at school.

Miss White interrupted the boys' conversation. "Caleb, I would like to meet with you at lunch today."

"Sure!" responded Caleb. He loved having lunch in the classroom, especially with his favorite teacher.

"Can I come, too?" asked Matt.

"Maybe another time, Matt. Today I just need Caleb," she answered.

"Not fair!" complained Matt.

They all laughed as Miss White messed up their hair.

During lunch, Caleb and Miss White sat at the round table in the back of the room. The classroom was quiet since everyone else was outside. As Caleb started eating his chicken nuggets, he watched his teacher unload her lunch bag. He always wondered what teachers ate. She had leftover pizza, an apple, and a bottle of water. Caleb loved pizza. He would eat it every day if he could.

"I've noticed that sometimes you seem worried or nervous in class," said Miss White.

"Yeah, my mom tells me I'm like that at home too," Caleb said in agreement. He told Miss White about the test and some of his other worries.

"I think I have something that will help you." She placed a jar in front of him. Across the top were the words, **Worries, worries in the jar.** "Have you ever heard of a worry jar?"

"No. What's that for?" Caleb asked.

"You write your worry down and put it into the jar. When you give the worry to the jar and you start to think about it again, you repeat the words, 'Worries, worries in the jar.' Let me show you. Tell me something that you're worried about."

"Finding a seat on the bus," explained Caleb. "But a worry jar will not help with that problem."

"You mean there are not enough seats on your bus?" questioned Miss White.

"No, no....You see, there's this girl named Kim who likes to be mean," explained Caleb. "I try to sit

worries, worries in the jar

as far away from her as I can so she leaves me alone."

"If she's mean, why don't you talk to the bus driver?" she suggested.

"Well, he does yell at her, but she just finds a way to do it when he's not looking."

"Okay, let's start with that," she said as she reached for a small white paper from the stack in her top desk drawer. "On the paper write, *finding a seat on the bus,* fold it up, and put it in the jar." Caleb followed her directions.

She continued explaining about the worry jar. "You identified your worry; now you need to let it go." On the board she wrote:

- Identify the worry
- Write it down and put it in the jar
- Then say the words, "Worries, worries in the jar"
- Don't think about what everybody else is doing
- Say, "I can do this"
- Then let the worry go

"How do I let it go?" questioned Caleb.

"That part will take some work. Kids worry about many things such as grades, friends, how they look, being liked…only you can control what you think. What you say to yourself is what you believe. For example, if you tell yourself over and over that you don't have any friends, you'll never make any. If you change your thinking to, I'll meet new kids and make new friends, then you'll make it happen. You're worried about finding a seat on the bus. So when was the last time you had to sit next to Kim?" she asked.

He looked up at the ceiling and then down at his tray. "Well, only one time this year."

"Only once?" Miss White asked.

Caleb felt a little embarrassed and nodded.

"You're causing yourself all of this worry and every day, except once, you found a seat away from Kim. When you tell yourself, I might have to sit next to Kim, you believe it and worry. It seems to me that this is something that you can work through and solve."

Caleb shrugged.

"As soon as you start to think about getting on the bus today, repeat the words, 'Worries, worries in the jar. I can do this,'" Miss White said. "Better yet, say the words and follow it with, 'I'll find a safe seat.'"

"Okay," Caleb replied.

"I'll tell you a story. When I was growing up, it took me a long time to learn to ride my bike because I was always worried about falling. We had a small hill in our backyard. My dad would hold onto my bike, I would get on, and he would let go. I was so afraid to try and ride the bike that I would just fall off."

Caleb laughed.

"Sounds funny, huh?" she said, as she laughed along. "Well, one day, let me see, it was a holiday weekend. I was excited for the afternoon because we were going to a picnic. However, there was still time to practice riding before we were planning to leave, so my dad had me back on that hill. I remember the phone rang and he let go of me to run in and answer it. As I started down the hill, I wasn't even thinking about pedaling and that's when it happened. I was riding my bike! When I stopped thinking about being afraid, I was able to balance, pedal, and ride my bike."

"It's hard not to be afraid," sighed Caleb.

"It sure is, Caleb. But many of the things that we worry about are things that we can teach ourselves to work through. The worry jar is one way to start. When you write the worry down, you give it away. Then you can start thinking positive thoughts instead of negative ones. This takes some practice, so let's start with finding a seat on the bus."

"Okay. I'll try today," he said.

That afternoon, as Caleb stood in line to get on the bus, he saw Kim standing in the front of the line. Into his head popped the thought of having to sit next to her. He started to panic but then remembered that the worry was in the jar.

I will get a seat. I don't have to worry. It's not working.... What are the words? Oh, worries, worries in the jar. I will find a safe seat.

Caleb probably repeated those words twenty times.

Kim went directly to the back of the bus, so there were plenty of seats away from her.

"Good afternoon, Caleb," Frank said.

"Hi, Frank," replied Caleb.

Finding a seat two rows behind the bus driver still allowed Caleb to look in the big mirror to see what Kim was up to.

"Can I sit with you?" asked Lucas.

"Sure," said Caleb.

Caleb saw a picture of a black dog on Lucas's

key chain.

"Is that your dog?" asked Caleb.

"Yes, his name is Jockey," he replied.

"I have a black dog that looks almost like that, but his name is Max," said Caleb.

The boys talked about their pets until it was time for Caleb to get off the bus. They were so busy talking that Caleb forgot all about Kim.

"See you tomorrow, Lucas," said Caleb.

"'Bye, Caleb," he said.

Did it work? At least this time it did…I think.

Chapter 4

It was Friday and another test for Caleb and his worry jar. He stood on the corner of his block waiting for the school bus. The sound of screeching brakes made Caleb immediately start thinking about where he would sit. His hands started to sweat and his heart started beating faster. When he looked up, he saw it was only the trash truck. *Whew! That was a close call,* Caleb thought. But the bus would be here soon.

It was time...worries, worries in the jar, Caleb thought. He started pacing back and forth on the sidewalk.

Worries, worries in the jar. I can do this. I will find a safe seat. I always find a seat, he reminded himself.

Caleb heard brakes again and this time it was the bus.

Worries, worries in the jar. I can do this.

When the doors opened, Frank said, "Good morning, Caleb."

"Good morning, Frank," Caleb replied.

Caleb looked down the rows of seats when a waving hand caught his eye.

"Caleb," said Lucas.

Caleb walked down the aisle and sat next to Lucas.

"Hey. Thanks for saving me a seat," Caleb said.

As Lucas and Caleb talked, he could feel himself relax a bit. The bus was extra noisy this morning. It was so noisy that at the next stop sign Frank yelled at everyone to keep their voices down. However, that didn't stop Kim.

"Kim, that's enough!" yelled Frank. "Bring your stuff and have a seat in the front."

Caleb and Lucas looked at each other. PANIC! She would be sitting two seats in front of them. Caleb knew that was closer than either one of them wanted to be to Kim. Caleb peeked around the corner of his seat.

As Kim made her way to her new seat, she purposely banged her book bag on every kid in her path.

"OUCH!"

"Quit it!"

Other kids complained as she passed. How could anyone be so mean? Kim's book bag hit the back of Caleb's head.

Ouch!

Both boys didn't say much more the rest of the ride to

school. Caleb stared straight ahead, wanting to be sure he was ready if Kim was going to say something nasty.

Caleb couldn't wait to get into the classroom, which was busy with kids talking and laughing. He wished the bus were more like his classroom so that he could enjoy it more. Caleb walked his homework up to Miss White's desk.

"So, how did it go?" she asked.

"Terrible. I was still worried about finding a seat," admitted Caleb.

"That's okay. It takes time. Don't give up. Giving up is easy. Working through your worries is hard," she explained.

"It is," agreed Caleb.

"I'd like to talk about some more of your worries," she said.

"Can I bring my lunch down again?" asked Caleb.

Matt had now joined them at her desk.

"Sounds like a plan," said Miss White.

"Can I come this time?" Matt asked, butting in on the conversation.

"Maybe next time, Matt. Caleb and I still have some work to do," Miss White replied.

"What's the big secret?" he asked.

"No secret, just working on something,"

All morning Caleb watched the clock. When it was finally lunchtime, Caleb grabbed his lunch bag and sat at the back table.

"What other worries would you like to work on?" Miss White asked, taking her lunch out of her bag.

"Math tests. They make me nervous," replied Caleb. He looked at her lunch, leftover pizza again? *I wish I could eat pizza as much as she did.*

"Why do they cause you to worry?" asked Miss White.

"Everyone else is way ahead of me. I'll never ever be as fast as them," explained Caleb.

"How do you have time to watch the other kids when you are supposed to be writing down answers?" she commented.

Caleb didn't know what to say, so he just shrugged.

"Are you worried about the test or the other kids?" she asked.

"I can almost do the entire test at home. I'm worried that I'm not as fast as everyone and they'll make fun of me," he explained.

"Did someone make fun of you?" she asked.

"Well, no." Caleb sighed as he lowered his head. "I guess I shouldn't worry about it, but it's hard to stop."

"That's what the worry jar will help you do," she explained. "So, can you put it into the jar?"

"I guess so," said Caleb.

Caleb wrote *Finishing the math test* on a slip of paper, folded it, and put it in the jar.

"What's next?" she asked.

"I worry about finding a seat at lunch. Well, at least when Matt's not here. I don't know where to sit," explained Caleb.

Caleb thought through his explanation because he was quickly learning that Miss White was going to ask him questions.

He continued. "Our class is last to get to lunch. By then, all of the tables are almost full. Matt and I can usually sit together, but when he's not here, I have to find a seat by myself."

"What exactly is your worry?" she asked.

"Um...finding a seat?" answered Caleb confused.

"Why are you worried about finding a seat?"

"Um...I get nervous sitting next to kids I don't know well," admitted Caleb.

"Well done!" Miss White said, holding up her hand for a high-five.

Caleb returned the high-five, but he didn't totally

understand what she meant. *Well done?*

"You may not realize how it works yet, but you will soon," she explained.

"First, write the worry down and put it into the jar. When you start to worry, say in your head, 'Worries, worries in the jar. I can do this.' Then forget about everyone else. This afternoon in math class, why don't you imagine that you are the only one in the room? Just answer the problems. When you start to look around, repeat the words, 'Worries, worries in the jar. I can do this' and focus on the next math problem."

Caleb nodded. "Does anyone else get distracted during tests, or is it just me?"

"Some do and some don't. I want to help you learn to refocus."

"Okay," Caleb replied, not really understanding.

"Do the same with finding a seat at lunch. When you think about finding a seat, say the words, 'Worries, worries in the jar. I can do this.' Then say, 'I can find a seat.' Plus, you may make a new friend," she suggested.

Caleb wrote the worries on the papers and put them in the worry jar.

Would he be able to keep his worries in the jar this time?

Chapter 5

Will I ever finish?

Caleb felt himself getting nervous. He wrote his name on another math test and quickly flipped it over. It had been a couple of weeks since the math worry went into the jar, but Caleb still didn't finish.

The worry is in the jar. Concentrate on the test. Worries, worries in the jar. Ugh...I don't think this is working.

"What are you staring at?" asked Matt.

"This test," sighed Caleb.

"Just relax," suggested Matt.

"Easy for you to say. You always finish," said Caleb. *Doesn't anyone understand?*

Worries, worries in the jar.

Caleb repeated those words over and over.

"What are you saying to yourself?" Matt asked.

Caleb thought a minute before he answered. Did he want to tell him about the worry jar?

"It's just something Miss White taught me to say so that I wouldn't worry so much," he answered.

"Oh," said Matt.

"Ready, set, go!" announced Miss White. BEEP, the timer started.

Caleb only answered the first row of problems when he started to look around the room. Matt was working quickly.

Say the words, say the words...

Worries, worries in the jar.

His eyes refocused on his test and he began row two.

Eight times seven, nine times four. The answers were taking longer and longer to figure out. Again Caleb looked at Matt, who was halfway down the test. His eyes scanned the classroom while his hands became sweatier.

Worries, worries in the jar.

Caleb refocused on row three and answered problem after problem.

Worries, worries in the jar.

Caleb worked through row four. Nine times six...nine

times six...he couldn't think of the answer. UGH! He looked over at Matt.

Worries, worries in the jar. Oh, and I can do this!

Fifty-four! He continued answering the problems in the rest of the row.

"Worries, worries in the jar. I can do this," he repeated to himself.

Row five was next. Five times five equals twenty-five. Eight times two equals sixteen. Four times seven equals twenty-eight. Six times nine...six times nine equals fifty-four. Caleb finished another row. The test was almost as exhausting as running laps in gym class.

Worries, worries in the jar. I can do this.

One by one, Caleb answered each problem. He looked up again. Matt was almost finished!

Worries, worries in the jar! Don't look up! Worries, worries in the jar. I can do this!

Row seven was easier, until nine times six. Again! Fifty-four!

Worries, worries in the jar. I can do this!

As soon as Caleb read the problem on row eight, he heard his classmates turn their papers over. He looked up to see who was finished. Then the timer went off. Caleb felt exhausted and frustrated, until he looked down at his paper. He smiled. Row eight! He had never made it to row eight at school before. Two more rows and he would have finished the whole thing.

Miss White was at her desk, so Caleb went directly over to her because he was so excited to share his paper.

"Miss White, look!" exclaimed Caleb.

"Row eight. What an improvement! I'm so proud of you," she said.

"I was nervous, but I kept repeating 'Worries, worries in the jar.' Then I told myself, 'I can do this.' During the test, I looked around the room and started to panic. So, I said, 'Worries, worries in the jar.'"

"Caleb, slow down," interrupted Miss White, and she laughed.

He was so excited. "I actually had to say it fifty times until I snapped out of it, but I didn't give up. Just like you said. Can I take this paper home to show my mom?"

"You sure can, Caleb! She will be so thrilled," answered Miss White, grabbing a pen. She graded Caleb's test so that he could take it home.

As soon as he got off the bus, Caleb ran into the house.

"Hey, Mom! Where are you?" Caleb yelled, as he went from room to room.

"I'm upstairs putting away the laundry," she replied.

"Look! Look at this!" yelled Caleb. He jumped up on the bed.

Caleb's mom looked over the math test and a huge smile spread across her face.

"All right! I am so proud of you!" she said, as she hugged him tightly.

Caleb broke free and jumped up and down on the bed.

"Hey! No jumping," instructed his mom.

"I can't help it. It's a great day!" sang Caleb.

He sat up. "You know what? At first I kind of thought the worry jar was silly, but now I like using it," admitted Caleb.

He looked out the bedroom window and thought about other things the jar helped him through. To start, Caleb no longer worried about finding a seat on the bus. That meant getting to school was much more relaxing.

Caleb had also added things like riding the roller coaster.

"I asked if I could put *any* worries in the jar and Miss White said yes! Anything can go in."

Caleb lay on the bed and hugged the pillow.

"I headed straight over to my worry jar. I wrote *riding the roller coasters.*" He rolled down to the bottom and somersaulted off the bed.

"Careful, Caleb."

"I walked back over to her and showed her the piece of paper and she laughed. I told her Kevin would call me chicken if I didn't get on this year." Caleb jumped back on the bed. "You know I'll be tall enough to get on every ride!"

"Caleb, please settle down."

"Mom, do you think I should tell my friends about the worry jar?"

"I don't see why not. What are you thinking?" asked Mom.

"Matt has been very worried about his karate belt test. I thought if he had a worry jar maybe it would help him too."

"That's a great idea. As a matter of fact, there are probably a lot of people who could use a worry jar," said Mom.

"Really?" asked Caleb.

"You're not the only one, honey. In fact, many grown-ups worry," she explained.

I never thought about grown-ups.

The weekend went by quickly, and the next week Caleb hoped that he would finally finish the whole math test.

"Arghhhh…," growled Caleb as the timer went off.

"How far did you get?" Matt asked.

Caleb showed his paper to Matt. "I made it to the last row! This is my best yet."

"Cool. So what secret did Miss White teach you? Could ya teach me so I can pass my belt test?" asked Matt.

"I worry a lot, so Miss White gave me a worry jar. I write down things I'm worried about and put them in the jar."

"A worry jar?" asked Matt.

"Yeah. When I panic, I say, 'Worries, worries in the jar. I can do this,' so I can focus on finishing the test.

Each day I get closer to finishing."

"Huh? I don't get what you're saying," said Matt.

"It's getting rid of worries. I used to worry about finding a seat on the bus. I didn't want to sit next to that fifth grader, Kim."

"I wouldn't want to have to sit next to Kim either," agreed Matt. "She's mean."

"I've never actually had to sit next to her. I always made sure to sit in a seat far away from her. So I put the worry in the jar to get rid of it. Then when I got nervous at bus time, I would remind myself that it was there and I'd say the words, 'Worries, worries in the jar' and 'I will find a safe seat.'"

"Worries, worries in the jar," repeated Matt. "It sounds silly to me."

"Don't forget 'I can do this.' I'm just saying, it helped me, so maybe it can help you," explained Caleb.

"I'll think about it," said Matt.

Chapter 6

The following week, Caleb and his mom pulled into the parking lot of the karate studio. Caleb ran ahead to see if Matt was inside. As the kids arrived, they talked together at the back of the room. Tracey and Madison were practicing their routines. Todd and his brother, Jason, waved goodbye to their parents. All ten kids were lined up, waiting for class to begin.

"You ready?" Caleb asked Matt. He heard Matt's stomach rumble.

Matt put his hand over his stomach. "I'm hungry, but I didn't eat dinner because I'm so nervous."

"Did you practice?" asked Caleb.

"Yeah, I did, but I'm worried I won't pass." Matt sighed.

"You should really try the worry jar," Caleb reminded Matt.

"I did. After you told me about it, I made one," admitted Matt.

"You did?" asked Caleb. He was surprised that his friend took his advice. "Awesome!"

"Yep, it's in my room, but I didn't put anything in it yet because I didn't know what to write," he explained.

Caleb glanced back at the doors of the karate studio. His mom was still standing there talking to Madison's mom.

"I'll be right back," Caleb told Matt.

"Hi, honey," said Caleb's mom.

"Hey there, Caleb," said Madison's mom.

"Hi, Mrs. D. Hey, Mom, do you have a pen and a small piece of paper?" asked Caleb.

"Let me check," she answered as she searched through her purse. It didn't take her long to find it. She was very organized. "Here you go, honey."

"Thanks, Mom!" He quickly ran back to Matt.

"Here, write your worry on the paper and I'll hold onto it," explained Caleb. He was really excited about helping Matt.

"What do I write?" asked Matt.

"What are you worried about?" asked Caleb, trying to remember some of the questions that Miss White had asked him.

"I won't get my belt," replied Matt.

"Are you worried about the test? I thought you knew all the moves," said Caleb.

Matt was quiet while he took off his shoes. More kids came into class. He looked around the room. "I'm more worried about messing up in front of everyone," admitted Matt.

"Write down the words *testing in front of everyone*," coached Caleb. Matt filled out the piece of paper. "Tell yourself the worry is in the jar. Then say, 'I'll pass the test.'"

"The worry is in the jar. I'll pass the test," repeated Matt. "It didn't work. I'm still nervous."

"No, no, no. It takes time," explained Caleb. "Listen, just try it. Miss White helped me. As soon as you start to feel nervous, say the words, 'Worries, worries in the jar. I can do this.' You have to keep saying it."

"Ladies and gentlemen, let's get started," announced the karate teacher, Bill. He checked his clipboard.

"We'll start with those who need to test for their orange belts. Let's see. Matt, are you ready?"

"Ready or not," Matt whispered to Caleb. He stood up front next to Todd at the mat. Both boys looked a little worried.

Caleb watched Matt walk out to the middle of the floor. He turned around and looked at Caleb. Caleb held

up the piece of paper and nodded. Matt nodded back.

"Come on, Matt, you can do it," Caleb said to himself.

He watched his friend step by step. Zack came over and sat next to Caleb on the floor.

"How's he doing?" Zack asked.

"So far, so good," replied Caleb.

Tracey, Madison, Todd, and Jason all joined the boys on the floor.

"How's he doing?" asked Todd.

"He looks good so far," replied Zack.

Matt looked over at Caleb. Once again, Caleb held up the folded paper, smiled, and gave him a thumbs-up.

Matt's last routine ended and everyone cheered when Matt joined the group.

"I passed!" he yelled.

"No worries," said Caleb.

"It worked," said Matt.

"What worked?" asked Taylor.

"The worry jar," explained Matt.

"What's a worry jar?" asked Todd.

"Yeah, I have worries," added Madison. "I wanna know too."

"The worry jar helped me to control my worries. Miss White taught me," Caleb started to explain. "She gave me a worry jar and I write down the things I'm worried about and put them in the jar. Then I do two things. First, I remind myself the worry is in the jar. Then, I tell myself I can do it. I say the words, 'Worries, worries in the jar. I can do this,' so I can relax a little."

"I don't get it," said Jason.

"I didn't get it either, but it's one of those things that you have to try," explained Caleb. "I used to worry about taking the math fact test. I learned that I was really worried about what other kids would say if I wasn't as good as them. So I put the worry in the jar. As soon as I started panicking and watching everyone else, I would remind myself the worry was in the jar. Then I would say, 'Focus on the math test.'"

"Maybe I need a worry jar so I don't panic about the spelling test," said Taylor.

"I'm worried about my saxophone solo that I'll perform in the spring concert next week," said Todd. "I need one too!"

"I've been worrying about my belt test tonight," Matt added. "I must have said, 'Worries, worries in the jar' five hundred times, but look at this." Matt held up his orange belt. "I owe this to the worry jar!"

Everyone laughed.

Caleb couldn't wait to go to school the next day. He wanted to tell Miss White about Matt and how everybody wanted a worry jar. Maybe everyone should have a worry jar. *She will be so proud of me.*

"Nothing could be too big for the worry jar!" Caleb gave Matt a high-five.

Chapter 7

When Caleb arrived at school the next day he was disappointed to see there was a substitute teacher. *Where is Miss White?* He went about his morning routine. Matt sat down beside Caleb at his desk.

"Hey, Caleb," said Matt. He had his belt on top of his desk.

"We have a substitute," reported Caleb.

"Oh...I wanted to show Miss White my belt," said Matt. "I guess I'll put it back in my book bag and show her tomorrow."

"I wonder where she is," said Caleb.

The day seemed to drag on without Miss White.

That night, Caleb's mom got a telephone call. She

went into the bathroom where Caleb was brushing his teeth.

"Caleb, when you're finished brushing, I need to talk to you about something," said his mom.

"I'll be right there," mumbled Caleb with a mouthful of toothpaste.

Caleb walked to his room and saw his mom sitting on the edge of his bed. By the look on her face, he could tell that she was upset about something.

"Come sit down," she instructed.

Caleb sat next to her and she put her arm around him. He didn't know what she was about to tell him, but he started to feel like it wasn't anything good. As a matter of fact, Caleb's stomach started to feel sick. *Did something bad happen?*

"Caleb, I just got a call from your school," she said. "Miss White was in an accident and she's in the hospital."

"What? Is she okay?" asked Caleb.

"They're not sure yet. When they find out more information, they'll let us know," she replied.

Caleb felt his eyes fill up with tears. He put his head down so his mom couldn't see, but somehow she knew and wrapped her arms around him. "Oh, honey, it's okay.

Let's wait for more information."

They sat together for a couple minutes without saying anything. Finally his mom asked, "Why don't you get ready for bed and I'll be back to tuck you in?"

He opened his dresser drawer and got out his favorite blue and green striped pajamas. All of a sudden the phone rang and Caleb ran downstairs to find out if it was the school.

"Hi, Linda. Yes, I heard the news. I guess we just have to wait until we hear more. Sure. Goodnight."

"Was it school? Is she okay? What did they say?" questioned Caleb.

"That was Matt's mom. We don't know any more information at this time. Miss White's family will contact Principal Vern when they hear from the doctors. All we can do is wait. It's getting late. Let's get you to bed," said Mom.

Caleb tossed and turned all night long, worrying about his teacher.

Caleb awoke and sat up in bed. The clock on the stand

next to his bed read two o'clock. He lay back down and put the pillow over his head.

Caleb lay there and wondered what kind of accident Miss White had been in. He closed his eyes real tight to try to fall back asleep. When he rolled over to look at the clock it said three o'clock in the morning.

Could there be a mistake?

Caleb sat up in bed again. He looked at the clock, which now read four thirty. His mind raced with more worry. He was frustrated and tired because he couldn't sleep. He was sad because he didn't know anything more about his teacher. Just then it hit him…maybe it would help. Caleb went over to his desk, grabbed a piece of paper, and wrote *Miss White*. He folded it in half and left it on his desk.

As he pulled the covers tight around him he said the words, "Worries, worries in the jar. Worries, worries in the jar."

He lost track of how many times he said those words over and over because the next thing he knew it was time to wake up.

Caleb quickly dressed. As soon as he got downstairs he asked his mom, "Did you hear anything?"

"Not yet," replied his mom. "Hopefully we'll learn

more today. I know you're worried. I am too. You should add this worry to your jar."

"I already did. Last night, I kept having bad dreams, so I wrote it down," said Caleb. "Worries, worries in the jar."

"Yes, 'Worries, worries in the jar.' I'm proud of you, Caleb," she said and hugged Caleb tightly. "Keep your worry in the jar. I love you, honey."

When Caleb got to his classroom, he saw the substitute again at Miss White's desk. The classroom was a lot quieter today, and he wondered if everyone had heard there had been an accident.

Following the announcements, Principal Vern came into the classroom.

"Good morning, boys and girls," he began. "I have some news to share with you. Many of you know by now that Miss White was in an accident. We just heard from her family that she is going to be away from school for a little while in order for her to get better."

Some of the kids raised their hands.

"Will we be able to go visit her?" asked Brian.

"Not right now. We will have to wait," he answered.

"What's wrong with her?" asked Jen.

"We have to wait for the doctors to figure that out,"

he answered. "I don't have a lot of answers right now. What we can do is make her some get-well cards to send to the hospital."

Later that day, Caleb went to the worry jar that sat on the back shelf next to the windowsill. He touched it and closed his eyes, remembering the first day that Miss White introduced it to him. Caleb took off the lid, reached into his pocket, and pulled out a folded piece of paper. He unfolded the paper and read the words, *Get better, Miss White*. His eyes filled up with tears as he put his new worry into the jar. Caleb sat down next to the shelf and cried.

"Worries, worries in the jar. She just has to be okay. Worries, worries in the jar," Caleb kept repeating. Then, just like that, he stopped. He knew what he had to do. He realized what she would need to get better and he would give it to her.

That night, he shared his plan with his mom. She hugged him and helped him make a very special worry jar.

Miss White's injury would keep her out of school for the rest of the year. But Caleb and his class looked forward to their video chat with her each week. It made the days better as they watched their teacher get stronger. When she talked with them, Caleb smiled because on the table behind her sat the worry jar that Caleb had sent her, filling up with folded pieces of paper.

At the end of each conversation Miss White would say, "No worries, my friends."

Author Letter

Do you worry? Let's face it; our society is filled with more stressors than when our parents grew up. As an elementary school teacher, I saw more and more children come to school worried. They worried about everything: family, friends, clothing, money, grades, divorce. I used worry jars to help my students. The first jar was given to a boy in 2000. He successfully implemented the worry jar into his routine. In 2001, the same boy was faced with an opportunity that would turn the tables and he would send his teacher a worry jar.

This book was written to teach children how to handle their worries. It is a true story about a student and Miss White, the author. The story will entertain and

inform children about things they can and cannot control. Additionally, the story will give adults a platform
to use when talking to children about worrying. I have
used worry jars with young children through adults. It is
amazing what you can do if you are not afraid to try.
I hope that every child who reads *Go Away Worries!*
passes it along to help others.

Michelle White

Here's the note I received from the student who inspired
this story:

Dear Miss White,

Here is a worry jar that I made for you. Put all your
worries in the jar, if you have any. I hope you get better
soon. Everyone is worried about you. We all miss you and
can't wait to see you again.

About the Author

The inspiration for *Go Away Worries!* is based on actual events from the author's life. Michelle White has a PhD in Education and has taught at both the elementary and college level. She has successfully used worry jars for many years with both children and adults. Michelle is also the author of *New Opportunities and ScubAbility.* She enjoys sharing her motivational messages of overcoming obstacles to schools and organizations. Contact Michelle at www.michellemariewhite.com.

About the Illustrator

Megan D. Wellman grew up in Redford, Michigan, and currently resides with her husband, Brent, daughter, Kylee, two Great Danes, and a cat in Canton, Michigan. She holds a bachelor's degree in fine arts from Eastern Michigan University with a minor in children's theater. *Go Away Worries!* is Megan's tenth book. Her books include *Does This Make Me Beautiful?*, *Liam's Luck and Finnegan's Fortune*, *King of Dilly Dally*, *This Babe So Small*, *Lonely Teddy*, *Grandma's Ready*, *...and that is why we teach*, *Being Bella*, and *Read to Me, Daddy!* which are all available from Ferne Press.

What is a worry?

A worry is a thought that keeps happening that makes you feel anxious or distressed. We all worry at times. But it is that nagging feeling that reoccurs that develops into worries. This may cause physical disturbances, such as stomachaches or headaches.

Why do kids worry?

Everyone worries. While adults have learned the skills to handle them, kids have not. Kids worry when they are afraid or unfamiliar with a situation and do not realize that all they may have to do is write it down and get rid of it. Different worries are prevalent at various stages of a child's development and may include some of the following: going to school, friends, grades, homework, tests, family situations, illness, etc.

How can you use the worry jar in the classroom?

The worry jar will help kids learn a skill to deal with anxieties. Further, it will help kids identify their fears by writing them down. Figure out what is causing them. The words "Worries, worries, in the jar" become a reassuring mantra that reminds kids to let go of the worry. Following those words with positive self-talk, "I can do this," creates positive self-esteem. The worry jar can be used at all educational levels and start from individual jars to whole class jars.

Other strategies to support the worry jar.

Here are a few ideas that will help. You have more control than you think.

1. When a worry keeps coming back in your mind, you can write it down and put it in the worry jar and let the worry jar have it.

2. You can tell your mind to STOP whenever you hear the worry coming back. Say "STOP" and "GO AWAY." "I don't have time for you." Keep saying it over and over. Then think of something that makes you feel good like singing a song, hugging your pet, or taking a fun ride on your bike.

3. You can talk to someone about your worry. There are specially trained people who will listen and support you.